The Whodunit Detective Agency

The Hotel Mystery

GROSSET & DUNLAP
Published by the Penguin Group
Penguin Group (USA) LLC, 375 Hudson Street, New York, New York 10014, USA

USA | Canada | UK | Ireland | Australia | New Zealand | India | South Africa | China

penguin.com
A Penguin Random House Company

Original title: LasseMajas Detektivbyrå Hotellmysteriet
Text by Martin Widmark
Original cover and illustrations by Helena Willis

English language edition copyright © 2014 Penguin Group (USA) LLC.
Original edition published by Bonnier Carlsen Bokförlag, Sweden, 2002. Text copyright
© 2002 by Martin Widmark. Illustrations copyright © 2002 by Helena Willis.
Published in 2014 by Grosset & Dunlap, a division of Penguin Young Readers Group,
345 Hudson Street, New York, New York 10014. GROSSET & DUNLAP
is a trademark of Penguin Group (USA) LLC. Manufactured in China.

Library of Congress Cataloging-in-Publication Data is available.

ISBN 978-0-448-48068-8 (pbk)   10 9 8 7 6 5 4 3 2 1
ISBN 978-0-448-48069-5 (hc)   10 9 8 7 6 5 4 3 2 1

The Hotel Mystery

WITHDRAWN

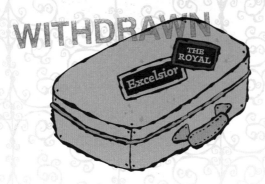

Martin Widmark
illustrated by Helena Willis

Grosset & Dunlap
An Imprint of Penguin Group (USA) LLC

The Hotel Mystery

The books in *The Whodunit Detective Agency* series are set in the charming little town of Pleasant Valley. It's the kind of close-knit community where nearly everyone knows one another. The town and characters are all fictional, of course . . . or are they?

The main characters, Jerry and Maya, are classmates and close friends who run a small detective agency together.

MUSEUM STREET
Museum
M
PLEASANT VALLEY SCH
News
Church
CHURCH STREET
Post Office
The Jeweler
HOT DOG
The Whodunit Detective Agency Headquarters

Jerry

Maya

Ronnie
Hazelwood

Bert
Anderson

Rita
Henderson

Pierre
Chalottes

The Braeburn family:

Mrs. Braeburn

Mr. Braeburn

Pippin

Winston

CHAPTER 1

The Day Before Christmas Eve

Every year, on the day before Christmas Eve, nearly everyone in the little town of Pleasant Valley does the same thing: They all head to the holiday buffet at the town's hotel, where they find turkey, ham, roasted carrots, and mashed potatoes and gravy, all served on big platters in the beautiful dining room.

This year, one of the holiday guests was Roland Sussman, the caretaker of the church just down the street. Like many others in town, he had the day off and was going to enjoy the buffet in the hotel. Roland brushed a few snowflakes off his coat, scarf, and hat before handing them to the coatroom attendant.

"Happy holidays, Mr. Sussman!"

Roland Sussman looked up in surprise.
There, in reception, was someone he knew:
Jerry! The young man and his binoculars had
once used the church tower as a spy
lookout. Jerry had said he was
looking for a rare bird,
but in fact he was
solving a tricky
case involving
stolen diamonds
at the jeweler's
shop across
the street.

"What a surprise to see you, Jerry! Are you working here? There can't be any rare birds at the hotel." Roland Sussman laughed.

"I'm working here during the winter break to help my uncle. Mostly, I help in the coatroom. But sometimes I run errands, carry suitcases to the rooms, or am here in reception."

"And your partner, Maya? How is she? I read all about the two of you in the newspaper after you solved the diamond mystery."

"Maya's here, too. She's helping in the kitchen."

"Do you have any exciting new cases in the works?"

Jerry shook his head.

"No? Well, the holiday buffet's waiting," Roland Sussman said with a smile. "Happy holidays to you and Maya," he said, and disappeared into the crowded dining room.

As he watched Roland walk away, Jerry thought about Maya.

The two of them were best friends and classmates at school, and together they ran the Whodunit Detective Agency. Their office was in Maya's basement. There, they kept everything they needed for their detective work: a pair of

WITH FLASH binoculars, a camera, several mirrors, flashlights, and a magnifying glass. They even had their own computer now. Jerry's and Maya's parents were friends, too, and had gone away for a couple of days together. They wouldn't be home until Christmas Day. Jerry and Maya had each begged their parents to be allowed to stay at home.

"We need to take care of the detective agency," said Jerry.

"We have to set up the computer," Maya said.

In the end, their parents agreed. After all, they could celebrate Christmas when their parents returned. Jerry and Maya were staying with Jerry's uncle Larry. He worked at the town's hotel on Market Square, and when he asked if they'd like to help out at the hotel for a few days, Jerry and Maya said yes. Perhaps something exciting would happen!

"Hi, Jerry! Has anything happened?"

It was Maya, who had just dropped by. She was on her lunch break and was taking the opportunity to look around the hotel, in true detective style.

"No, nothing special,"

replied Jerry. He could see that she was disappointed. Maya was always on the hunt for an interesting assignment for their detective agency.

"Oh well," she said. "Anyhow, the hotel manager wants to talk to us in his office at 4:00 p.m. He's going to tell us about the holiday celebrations and a very important family that's arriving at the hotel tomorrow."

"Okay," said Jerry. "I'll see you there."

CHAPTER 2

VIP Guests

At four o'clock in the afternoon, the hotel manager's office was full of people. The manager, Ronnie Hazelwood, was a man of about fifty. He had long muttonchops on his cheeks, but not a hair on his head.

Ronnie had visited Pleasant Valley one fall day a few years ago. Although he had just come for a vacation by the water, when he saw a run-down hotel, he was charmed: He would buy the old hotel and fix it up. And a year later, the hotel was as good as new.

Jerry's uncle said the hotel manager had an iron will, a heart of gold, and a wallet as empty as an old mine. Fixing up the hotel must have cost him a couple million dollars.

Now, he had called the staff together around the big table in his office.

To the left of the kind manager sat grumpy Bert Anderson. Bert worked in reception. Jerry and Maya disliked him immediately. He bossed people around and acted like he owned the hotel. He made Jerry and Maya call him *sir.*

Jerry's uncle had told them that Bert Anderson spent all his time alone because no one wanted to be friends with a man who never smiled and was only interested in his stamp collection.

Here in the meeting, the moody receptionist noisily drummed his fingers on the table. Clearly, he didn't think he had time to sit there.

Next to the unpleasant Bert Anderson sat his complete opposite: the friendly

and always-cheerful Rita Henderson, a chef
from New Orleans. Jerry's uncle said that
the manager, Ronnie Hazelwood, had
a crush on Rita.

Rita dreamed of one
day opening her own
restaurant in France. But
she didn't have enough
money, and spent most
of her paychecks on
lottery tickets and
scratch cards, hoping
to win big. During
the meeting, she was
scratching a card with
a penny.

"Useless!" She laughed and ruffled Jerry's hair. "I didn't even win a dollar! But one day I'll hit the jackpot, and then I'll be off to France!"

Opposite friendly Rita sat Pierre Chalottes, a dark-haired and sad-looking housekeeper from France. Pierre didn't say much, but Jerry and Maya had noticed how he and Rita liked to sit together and whisper during their lunch breaks.

"Well, now," said Ronnie Hazelwood. "The hotel's holiday celebrations are under way." The manager's whole face lit up with a smile. "Maya is helping Rita bake a big gingerbread house, which will go in reception. First thing tomorrow morning, Jerry will decorate the tree in the lounge. We'll hand out the holiday presents there at 4:00 p.m. I'll dress up as Santa Claus—or do you think we should

have a reindeer this year? That could be
a part for you, Bert!"

The hotel manager chuckled and gave
Bert a friendly thump on the back. Maya
saw Bert's upper lip twitch slightly. Some
might have thought it was the beginning
of a smile, but Maya suspected it was more
of a snarl, and that Bert Anderson would
like to bite his boss's hand.

"Anyway," the hotel manager continued,
without noticing his receptionist's
annoyance, "tomorrow is not only Christmas
Eve, but also a very important day for the
hotel. The Braeburn family has reserved

the hotel's best suite. The family plans to stay for quite a while. This means a lot of money for the hotel, and goodness knows we certainly need it. We all must make sure that everything runs perfectly during their stay."

Jerry and Maya could see that the manager was nervous.

"Mr. and Mrs. Braeburn will be here with their daughter, Pippin, and a small dog, Winston."

The manager continued talking about the wealthy family: "Mr. Braeburn made it very clear that Winston is to receive the best treatment. Otherwise he could become stressed and stop eating. Evidently, the Braeburns own a very expensive and unusual dog, and nothing bad must happen to it," he firmly concluded.

"I'm sure everything will be fine with the dog. You'll see," Rita said with a laugh.

The hotel manager relaxed a little and gazed affectionately at Rita.

"Well, I think that covers everything," he said, and closed the meeting.

Then the staff members left the room and continued their preparations for the holiday celebrations.

CHAPTER 3

Short on Money

Christmas Eve morning arrived. It was a beautiful, sunny winter's day. The air was clear and cold, and the snow crunched as Jerry, Maya, and Uncle Larry walked through town. Inside the hotel foyer, it was cozy and warm. The smell of coffee and gingerbread filled the air.

Maya and Jerry said hello to grumpy Bert Anderson, who was sitting in reception leafing through a magazine about stamps. Maya remembered that Jerry's uncle had said that a very rare stamp was for sale, and that Bert Anderson couldn't afford to buy it. That was probably why he was in a particularly bad mood that day.

"Merry Christmas, Mr. Anderson!" Jerry and Maya said in unison.

Bert Anderson just grunted in reply, without lifting his eyes from the magazine.

The housekeeper, Pierre Chalottes, was arranging a beautiful bouquet of winter flowers. Seeing Pierre reminded Jerry of what had happened the previous afternoon, and he started chuckling. The mailman had announced that he had a package for "Pier Scallops"!

"It's French, and it's pronounced *Pee-air Sha-lot*," Jerry had to explain.

Pierre had opened the package in the break room. It contained cheese and crackers from France. Pierre's mother sent goodies to her son,

Pierre
Chalottes
Pleasant Valley
Hotel
United States

Cra

knowing that he was homesick. She sent
the care packages hoping they would lure
him back home to France.

Maya disappeared into the kitchen
and Jerry continued to the lounge. It
was time to decorate the big fir tree.
Uncle Larry came in with a huge box of
decorations, and Jerry got right to work.
He hung strings of lights, glass ornaments,
little snowmen, and strings of garland.
He delicately draped tinsel over the
branches. Hard at work behind the tree,
Jerry was almost completely hidden by
the branches and decorations.

After a few minutes, Jerry heard
some people come into the lounge.
He recognized their voices: It was Rita

and Pierre. They couldn't see Jerry behind the tree, and thought they were alone in the room. Rita didn't sound as cheerful as usual. On the contrary, she sounded upset.

"If we're going to open our own restaurant, we need $30,000," said Rita. "How are we ever going to get a hold of that kind of money?"

"But darling," began Pierre, "my mother said we could borrow the money from her."

"I refuse to borrow money from anyone. No, thank you! I'd rather stay here and work for someone else," Rita hissed angrily.

Rita and Pierre left the lounge.

On the other side of the hotel, Maya was standing in the hallway just outside the manager's office. She had stopped behind the open door. The manager was talking on the telephone and sounded agitated.

"I promise! You will have the money in the next few days," he said.

Ronnie Hazelwood sighed and hung up the phone. Maya walked by as if she had heard nothing.

CHAPTER 4

A Chinese Apple Dachshund

It was nearly noon, and the grand Braeburn family was due to arrive at any minute. The staff members stood at attention in reception. Then, in walked the family, right on time!

The elegant Mrs. Braeburn entered first, sweeping into the room draped in an expensive fur coat. Behind her came a short man who must have been Mr. Braeburn. And finally, in walked their daughter, Pippin. Mr. Braeburn carried a red velvet cushion. On the cushion sat the fattest dog Jerry and Maya had ever seen.

Now there's a dog that has never refused food, thought Maya.

She stretched out her hand to pet him.

But the dog, Winston, was surprisingly quick and not very friendly. He turned his plump head and snapped at Maya, who quickly recoiled. Pippin told everyone:

"Winston does not like to be touched by hotel staff. Chinese apple dachshunds are highly sensitive dogs. We have been offered $30,000 for him, but we have no intention of selling him."

Jerry looked around at the staff. The manager, Pierre, Rita, and Bert each had a gleam in their eyes, as if they were looking not at a beloved pet, but at a fat wad of dollar bills—a snuffling, slobbering wad of bills on a red velvet cushion. Jerry and Maya knew there were a lot of people in the hotel who would love to get their hands on that kind of money.

"We'll do everything we can to make sure you and your dog are happy here," said the groveling hotel manager. "In fact, this afternoon at four, we'll present gifts to all of the children in the lounge."

Snort and snuffle!

24

Jerry took one of the Braeburns' suitcases in each hand and climbed the stairs to their luxury suite. He read the address labels stuck on the cases. They were from five-star hotels in New York, Miami, and Chicago. *This family is clearly used to living in style and sparing no expense*, Jerry thought. He opened the door to room 13 and set down the suitcases.

At 4:00 p.m., the hotel guests and staff gathered by the fir tree. A lovely fire crackled in the fireplace. There was a knock on the door. It was the manager, dressed up as Santa Claus. Several of the young children gasped.

"Ho-ho-ho!" he chortled. "Are there any good children here?"

It was clear that the manager enjoyed dressing up as Santa and giving out presents. He wore a fluffy fake beard, a big red hat, and a red suit, and danced around the room with a sack of gifts. *None of the children will recognize me under this holiday costume!* he thought.

Pippin stood by the tree, tugging on a glass ornament.

"Here's a sweet little girl! I'm sure she's been very good this year," said the manager.

He tried to pat Pippin on the head, but she reached over and grabbed the package from Santa's hands. She ran across the floor and yelled: "Look, Mommy! Look what I got from that silly manager!"

The manager laughed nervously. He quickly gave out the rest of the presents and disappeared from the room.

Later that evening, the guests danced around the cheerily decorated tree and then enjoyed a special Christmas dinner in the large dining room. Ronnie Hazelwood had changed out of his costume and was sitting next to Mr. Braeburn.

"And how is your little dog? Has he made himself at home in the suite? Should we send up a tasty little sausage?"

"Winston doesn't eat after 6:00 p.m. He gets gas," replied Mr. Braeburn, taking a sip of the expensive wine he had ordered.

The manager nodded sympathetically.

Pippin threw the doll she got from the manager on the floor.

"Yuck! This food's disgusting," she said. "I want to watch TV."

"Of course, Pippin," replied Mrs. Braeburn. "We'll go up to the room soon. We have to make sure Winston is all right, don't we?"

Later, when all the guests had finally gone to bed, Jerry and Maya sat in the lounge. They shared some apple cider and enjoyed the peace and quiet.

Uncle Larry had gone home, and Jerry and Maya were about to go, too.

Then suddenly, they heard a scream from upstairs.

CHAPTER 5

The Dog Has Gone

Who had screamed? It sounded like Mrs. Braeburn. What had happened?

Jerry and Maya rushed out of the lounge and up the stairs. The hotel manager was also on his way up to the next floor. His hand was wrapped in a bandage spotted with blood! What had he done? But there was no time for questions.

Jerry, Maya, and the manager reached the hallway where the special guests were staying.

Suddenly, the door next to the Braeburn family's room opened and out walked Rita and Pierre! What were *they* doing in there?

The surprises continued: Bert Anderson walked down the hall with a smile on his face!

What in the world could have put that old grouch in a good mood?

Jerry and Maya looked at one another curiously. Every member of the staff seemed to be acting suspiciously this evening! The manager's bloodstained bandage, Rita and Pierre meeting in the room right next to

the Braeburns, and Bert Anderson in a good mood for once.

"There's something fishy going on," Jerry whispered to Maya. Before she had a chance to respond, the door to the Braeburns' suite burst open.

"Winston's gone!" howled Mrs. Braeburn.
"We've looked everywhere! He's nowhere
to be found in our suite. Our precious dog
has been stolen!"

Mr. Braeburn ran up and down the
hallway with the red velvet cushion in one

hand and a sausage in the other. He hoped
to lure the dog back.

After a while, he stopped, turned to the
hotel manager, and started to threaten him:
"If Winston isn't back here within the hour,
you'll be sorry!"

The hotel manager mopped sweat from his forehead, bowed down, and began to grovel. He promised that they would search the hotel from top to bottom. Rita, Pierre, the hotel manager, Bert, Jerry, and Maya all ran off in different directions. They searched every broom closet and guest room from the basement to the attic. But there was no sign of Winston.

An hour later, the hotel staff gathered outside the Braeburns' suite again.

The hotel manager, Ronnie Hazelwood, adjusted his bandage. He took a deep breath before knocking.

Mr. Braeburn flung open the door.

"Well . . . we have, er . . . um . . . haven't . . . ," mumbled the manager.

"You haven't found our dog!" roared Mr. Braeburn. "Disgraceful! We demand compensation for Winston. Our poor little dog has, no doubt, disappeared for good.

We will leave the hotel first thing tomorrow morning, and you should be thankful we aren't going to the police! The hotel can pay for the room."

Mrs. Braeburn tottered over. She leaned dramatically against the doorway and held her hand to her forehead.

"Naturally," groaned the manager.

Mr. Braeburn slammed the door with a bang.

It was a sad group that was left to say good night to one another in the hallway that evening. Maya and Jerry walked down the stairs, both deep in thought.

"Something doesn't seem right here," said Jerry. "I can feel it in my bones."

They entered the lounge again, where the fire had died down to mere embers. Jerry and Maya sat on the sofa and went over what they knew.

"A dog worth $30,000 has disappeared," began Jerry. "The dog couldn't have escaped from a locked hotel room, so he must have been stolen. Everyone on the staff knows that the master key, which opens all the rooms, hangs in the cabinet in reception. Who needs money the most?"

"The manager, Ronnie Hazelwood, needs money for this hotel," continued Maya. "And he has mysteriously hurt his hand. Did he take Winston? Did that snappy little dog bite the manager's hand as he was kidnapping him?"

"Rita and Pierre want to start a restaurant, and they need $30,000 to get started. What were they doing in the room next to the Braeburns? Were they listening through the wall, and did they creep in when everyone was asleep? Have they taken the dog to get the money for their dream project?" asked Jerry as he looked into the embers.

"Or is it Bert Anderson, the old grouch?" asked Maya. "Why was he suddenly in such a good mood? Did he take the dog? Nobody would find it easier to get ahold of the master key than he would. If he sells the dog, he could buy that stamp he wants so badly for his collection."

"There's something familiar about the Braeburn family," said Jerry thoughtfully.

"I've got an idea," said Maya. "Come with me!"

CHAPTER 6

Apples on the Net

Maya dragged Jerry through the darkened hotel, and finally came to the manager's office, where it was completely quiet. Maya reached for the door handle and, finding it unlocked, hurried them both inside. She went to the desk and switched on the manager's computer. It started with a hum.

"Let's search the Internet. There are millions of websites about different topics, so we should be able to find something to help us understand what's going on!"

"Good idea!" exclaimed Jerry.

"We'll search for each of the things we learned tonight," said Maya.

The first thing Maya typed was *Chinese*

apple dachshund. It took only a moment for the results: No results.

It seemed there was nothing on the Internet about a breed of dog called the Chinese apple dachshund.

"I'd say that if we can't find anything about the Chinese apple dachshund on the Internet, then it isn't a real breed of dog," said Maya.

"So you think the Braeburn family is lying about what kind of dog they have? But why?"

"I don't know yet. Let's keep searching. What else do we know about the family?" asked Maya.

"We know their names," said Jerry.

Maya typed in *Braeburn + Pippin + Winston* and clicked the search button.

Once again, the computer started to search, and two seconds later, a link appeared: *Popular apple varieties.*

"I knew it!" exclaimed Jerry. "I knew there was something familiar about their names. I've heard all those names before, but not for *people*. They are types of apples. Everyone in the family is named after a different kind of apple. Keep clicking, Maya!"

Maya clicked on the link, and a long list of apple varieties came up.

"Aha!" said Jerry. "Now we know that: (a) there is no breed of dog called the Chinese apple dachshund, and (b) everyone in the family has a name that matches a type of apple.

"But what do we do now?" he asked. "I'm sure that the Braeburns are planning some sort of scheme. We need to find some proof!"

He looked at Maya, who was spinning around on Ronnie Hazelwood's chair.

"We need more pieces of the puzzle," she said. "What else do we know?"

Jerry sighed. They seemed to have gotten stuck just as they thought they were about to solve the mystery.

"I know!" exclaimed Jerry. "We know they have stayed in hotels in New York, Miami, and Chicago."

"But how does that help us?" asked Maya.

"Don't you see?" said Jerry. "Let's run the entire list of apple names with *New York + Miami + Chicago*. The computer will find if there is any connection—a connection between the types of apples and the city names."

Jerry and Maya typed in everything and searched again. Now, a list of newspaper articles from New York, Miami, and Chicago came up.

"Bingo!" said Jerry.

They clicked on the newspaper articles, all of which appeared to be about an unusual family—a family that had lost its dog on various occasions in exclusive hotels across the country!

From various newspapers in New York, Miami, and Chicago, the links read:

[Lost Dog at the Grand Hotel in New York, Lord Lambourne's Family Distraught](#)

[Scandal at Luxury Hotel in Miami, James Grieve Family in Tears](#)

[Drama in Chicago:
Who Stole the Dog?
Mr. and Mrs. Macintosh
Have Lost Their Beloved Pet](#)

Jerry and Maya read each article. It looked as if the family traveled to luxury hotels and used a different name in each place. When it was time to check out, their "valuable" dog always disappeared. It was the same story in every city. The family in room 13 was a fraud. But now they had been found out!

Jerry and Maya looked at one another. Now it was just a matter of tricking the family into giving itself away. They switched off the computer and crept quietly out of the hotel.

They made their way home through the dark, empty streets, with the soft glow of holiday decorations lighting the way. Their eyes were heavy from lack of sleep. But now they knew what they had to do in the morning!

CHAPTER 7

In a Red Case

The Braeburn family was planning to leave the hotel that morning. Around 9:00 a.m., the hotel manager, Ronnie Hazelwood, came downstairs. He walked with heavy steps: He had not slept much the night before.

Maya and Jerry explained what they had learned and told him their plan. Ronnie Hazelwood beamed with joy.

"Excellent work! You've saved the hotel!" he exclaimed. "I'll ask the police chief to come immediately."

A little later, the Braeburn family came downstairs. Mr. Braeburn carried a big red suitcase. Mrs. Braeburn was sobbing, and Pippin was looking down at the floor. Jerry and Uncle Larry fetched the other suitcases from room 13.

When everything was ready, Mr. Braeburn said:

"My family is heartbroken. We didn't sleep a wink last night. We miss our beloved little dog. I don't think your money can ever make up for our sorrow. But I do understand if you insist on paying our bill so that you'll feel as if you've done the right thing."

The hotel manager had to hide under the counter to keep his huge smile from showing.

But when he stood up again, he had pulled himself together.

"An express letter came for you this morning, *Lord Lambourne*," he said.

The manager held out the letter. Mr. Braeburn put down the red suitcase and took the letter without saying anything about being called *Lord Lambourne*. Jerry and Maya could barely keep still. He had walked straight into the trap!

Mr. Braeburn tore open the letter. It said:

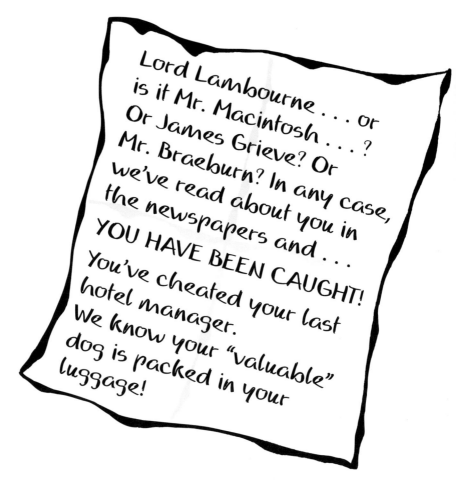

Lord Lambourne . . . or
is it Mr. Macintosh . . . ?
Or James Grieve? Or
Mr. Braeburn? In any case,
we've read about you in
the newspapers and . . .
YOU HAVE BEEN CAUGHT!
You've cheated your last
hotel manager.
We know your "valuable"
dog is packed in your
luggage!

The man with the many apple names
staggered backward. His wife looked at
him, horrified. He bumped into the red
suitcase and it wobbled. From inside came
a muffled *woof*!

Mr. Braeburn looked around in bewilderment.

"We wrote that letter," said Maya. "And I'm guessing your beloved little dog is inside that suitcase there," she continued, nodding toward the red suitcase.

"Watch what you say, child!" hissed Mrs. Braeburn. "How dare you suggest such a thing? You think we would lock our own little darling in a suitcase?"

Her outburst was followed by another *woof*! Mr. Braeburn opened the case, and sure enough, there was Winston, fat and drowsy. A disgusting smell wafted through the hotel foyer.

Presumably, the dog had been given tranquilizers to keep him quiet. Next to him was a half-eaten sausage.

It seems like the only true thing the Braeburns said was that their dog passed gas, thought the hotel manager.

Just then, the police chief came through the hotel entrance.

"Aha!" he said, wrinkling his nose at the smell. "The hotel manager explained everything to me on the phone. It seems we have a case of a lost dog and an attempt to cheat the hotel out of a lot of money."

The police chief pointed to the dog.

"Here is the missing pooch, and I presume these are the criminals," he continued, fixing his gaze on the Braeburn family.

Pippin crouched down next to the dog and petted him. Winston panted heavily and farted.

The hotel employees watched as the police chief escorted the gloomy family out of the hotel.

The minute the doors closed behind them, celebrations broke out.

The manager, Ronnie Hazelwood, looked happily at his staff, and then at Jerry and Maya. "Thank you, Jerry and Maya! You have saved me and the entire hotel from disaster."

CHAPTER 8

Truth Revealed

The hotel manager smiled at Jerry and Maya.

"I promise that you can eat at the holiday buffet free of charge—for the rest of your lives!" But then he fell silent, because there were still a number of questions unanswered.

The hotel manager turned to Rita and Pierre.

"Why were you meeting in room 14 last night?"

Everyone turned to Rita and Pierre. Pierre looked at his feet, and Rita blushed all over.

"We love each other," said Rita finally. "And we want to get married, move to France, and open a restaurant." Rita's blush turned into a smile.

That made the hotel manager smile, too!

Then Ronnie Hazelwood turned to Bert Anderson.

"And what about you, Bert—why did you look so pleased with yourself yesterday evening?"

The strange grin came back to Bert Anderson's face.

"The stamp was burned," he began. "The store that was selling the stamp caught fire last night."

"But I thought you really wanted that particular stamp," said the manager.

"Oh, I did! Nothing would please me more. But if I can't have it, I don't want anyone else to, either."

The hotel manager shook his head. Bert
Anderson was strange and always would be.
But that didn't make him a criminal.

"And now, I bet you're all wondering
what I did to
my hand,"
said Ronnie
Hazelwood.
The manager
held up his
bandage.

"You probably thought that nasty little dog, Winston, had bitten me." The hotel manager laughed. "In fact, I just happened to cut myself on a broken glass when I was cleaning up the kitchen."

Now that the case was solved, the hotel staff could relax again. The manager offered everyone breakfast in the dining room. They were all talking at once about what had happened when, suddenly, there was a knock on the door. It was the church caretaker, Roland Sussman.

"Sorry to disturb you, but I wonder if I left my scarf when I came for the buffet yesterday? It is red and dotted with green apples," he said hesitantly.

"The only apples we know of are sitting in jail as guests of the police chief," the manager said with a smile.

Everyone in the dining room burst out laughing. Ronnie Hazelwood, Rita Henderson, Pierre Chalottes, Uncle Larry, Jerry, and Maya laughed until tears ran down their faces. Even grumpy old Bert Anderson allowed himself an uncharacteristic grin.

The caretaker, Roland Sussman, didn't understand what was going on, but he didn't really care as long as he got his scarf, which he did. After he left, the hotel staff returned to their usual tasks.

Once they were alone, the manager turned to Jerry and Maya.

"It's quite possible that there will be something in the paper about my hotel in the next few days. And that will be good for business. So, thank you, again," he said, and shook hands with the two detectives.

Outside, it had begun to snow. The peace of the holiday season finally fell upon the town and its little hotel.

And sure enough, the newspaper ran a story the very next day:

THE WHODUNIT AGENCY SOLVES YET ANOTHER CASE

With great observation skills and an excellent understanding of modern technology, a pair of young detectives, Jerry and Maya, have solved another complex case. This time, they caught a family of high-class frauds. The criminal family had been living in luxury in expensive hotels across the country. To avoid paying the hotel bills, the family faked the theft of their dog. Hotel managers in several states had allowed the family to leave without paying in order to avoid claims for compensation.

The police chief in Pleasant Valley has announced that the family is still, in a way, living free of charge, and that an airy backyard for a certain Chinese apple dachshund is urgently needed.

Coming soon!

The **Whodunit** Detective Agency

The Circus Mystery

Pickpockets and Ice Cream

It was summertime in the town of Pleasant Valley. The sun had been shining brightly all day, and a gentle breeze rustled through the leaves of the trees in town.

"Hi there, kids!" someone called out to Jerry and Maya as they bicycled down the street.

It was the police chief, who was standing in front of a little newspaper stand enjoying an ice-cream cone. Jerry and Maya pedaled over to him. The police chief was an old acquaintance, and it was always good to talk to him.

"What a fantastic day," he said. "Perfect ice-cream weather, don't you think?"

"Absolutely," replied Jerry. "Maya and I are

Ice Crea

ICE CREAM
PRICE LIST

1 scoop $1
2 scoops $2
3 scoops $3

or

on our way to the beach for a swim."

"Lucky things," the police chief said with a laugh. "We poor police officers have to keep our noses to the grindstone day in and day out."

Jerry and Maya looked at each other and winked. The police chief didn't exactly seem overwhelmed with work.

"Have you been busy at the station?" asked Maya, curious all the same. The two friends ran a small detective agency together, and Maya was always on the lookout for an exciting new case.

"I really shouldn't tell you this," said the police chief. "But you have helped me before, and I'm sure you can keep a secret, can't you?"

Jerry and Maya nodded eagerly.

The police chief leaned forward and lowered his voice to a whisper. "Pickpockets! At the circus outside town! Several people were robbed at the first performance yesterday. I've called the police stations in the other towns where the circus has performed, and it's always the same thing: Cell phones, necklaces, and wallets disappear after each show."

The police chief nodded thoughtfully and continued, "But as soon as the circus leaves town, the thefts stop, too. It seems as if the thief is part of the circus."

The police chief leaned in even closer, and Jerry saw that the scoop of melting ice cream was about to plop right out of the waffle cone in the chief's hand. The police chief narrowed his eyes and whispered, "I'm going to the circus to check it out—in plain clothes, of course. It takes a trained eye like mine to spot a skilled pickpocket. I'm going to both shows this evening: the one at 6:00 p.m. and the one at 8:00 p.m."

With a splat, the chief's ice cream fell out of the cone and landed on the sidewalk. The police chief frowned at the sticky puddle at his feet, but before he could react, his cell phone rang.

The police chief answered it in a serious voice: "Hello. Police chief of Pleasant Valley speaking." Then he covered it with his hand and whispered to Jerry and Maya:

"What a coincidence! It's the ringmaster."

Jerry and Maya didn't want to interfere with official police business, so they waved good-bye and cycled on.

Just a block away at Market Square, Maya surprised Jerry by suddenly turning right instead of left.

"Wrong direction, Maya! The beach is this way."

"Forget the swim, Jerry! We have a job to do!"

Of course! Jerry understood exactly where Maya was heading: to the circus!

The Whodunit Detective Agency had a new case to solve.